To all those four-legged creatures who are looking for a home, to those who work tirelessly in finding those homes, and to those who open their hearts and homes to give them one.

All proceeds from the Webster the Beagle books go to local charities, little league teams, and the Children's Hospital in Richmond, Virginia.

www.mascotbooks.com

Webster the Beagle and His Adventures at the River

©2024 Frank Payne. All Rights Reserved. No part of this publication may be reproduced, stored in a retrieval system or transmitted in any form by any means electronic, mechanical, or photocopying, recording or otherwise without the permission of the author.

For more information, please contact:
Mascot Kids, an imprint of Amplify Publishing Group
620 Herndon Parkway, Suite 220
Herndon, VA 20170
info@mascotbooks.com

Library of Congress Control Number: 2023923517

CPSIA Code: PRKF0224A

ISBN-13: 978-1-63755-673-3

Printed in China

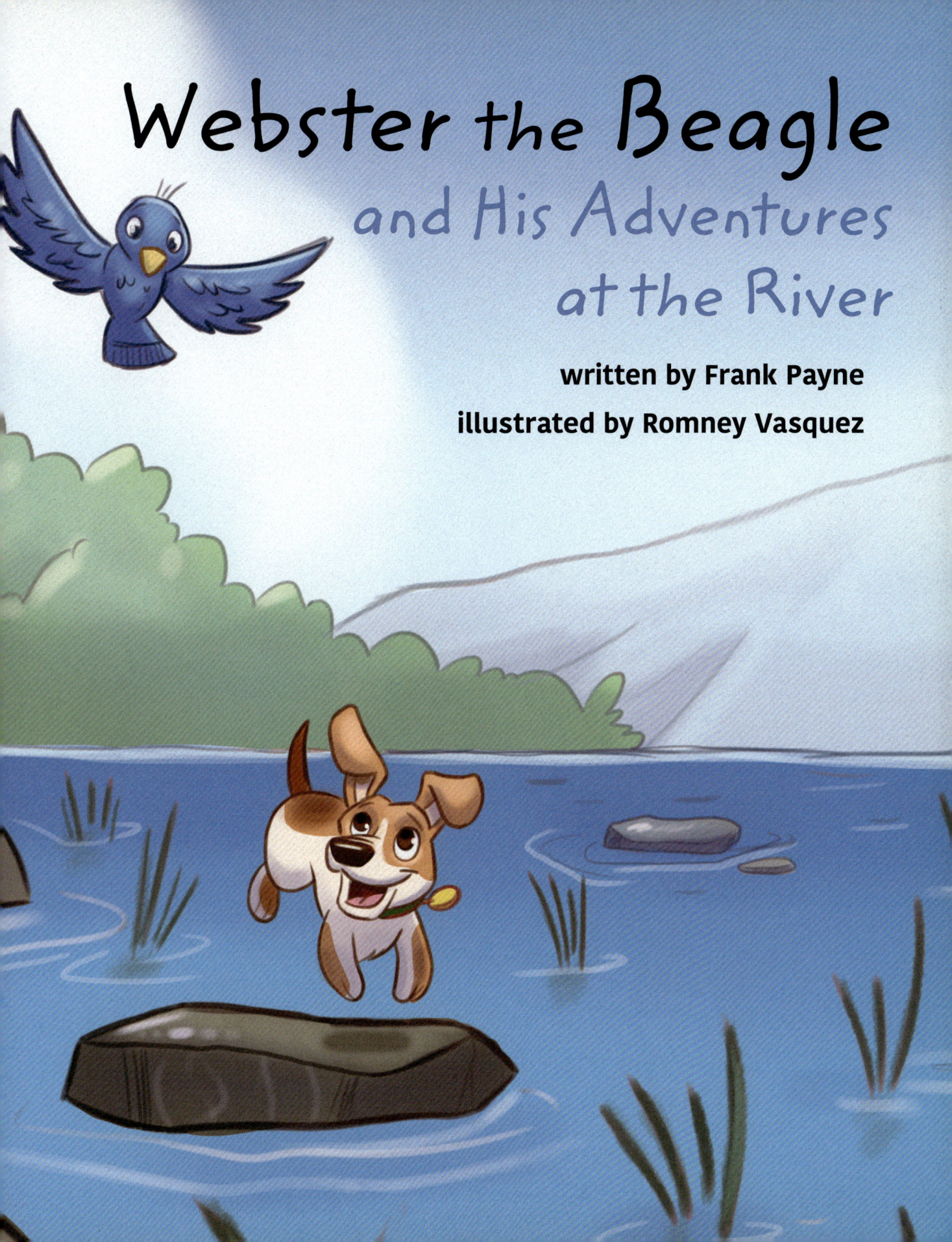

Webster the Beagle was a hunting dog who was born in a kennel with many other dogs. One day, Webster got lost while he was hunting.

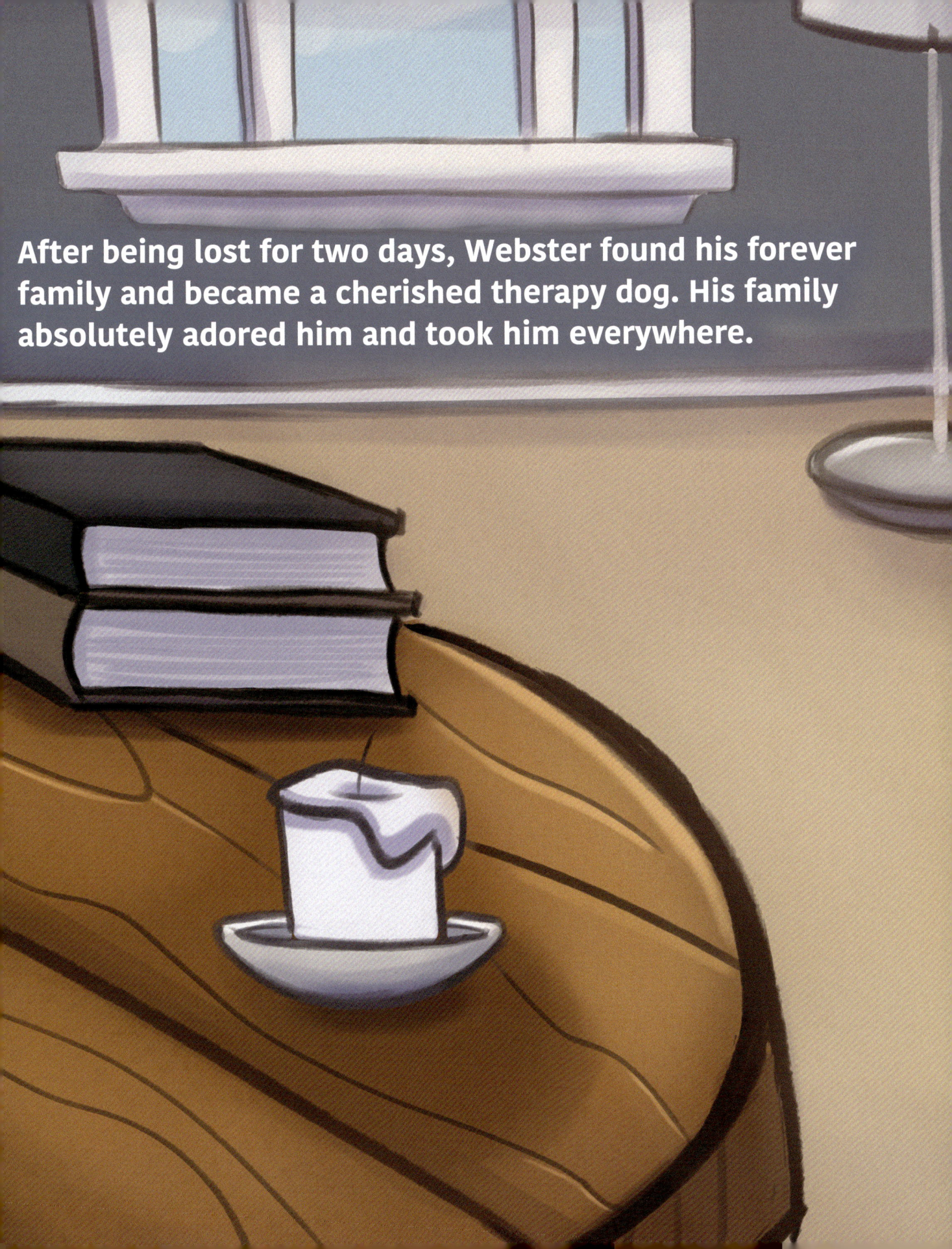

When he visited the river, he had numerous opportunities to see so many other critters that didn't look like him—they had feathers, shells, and fins! Webster was a former hunting dog, and he was excited to see all these new animals! He didn't need to chase them anymore—he could play with them!

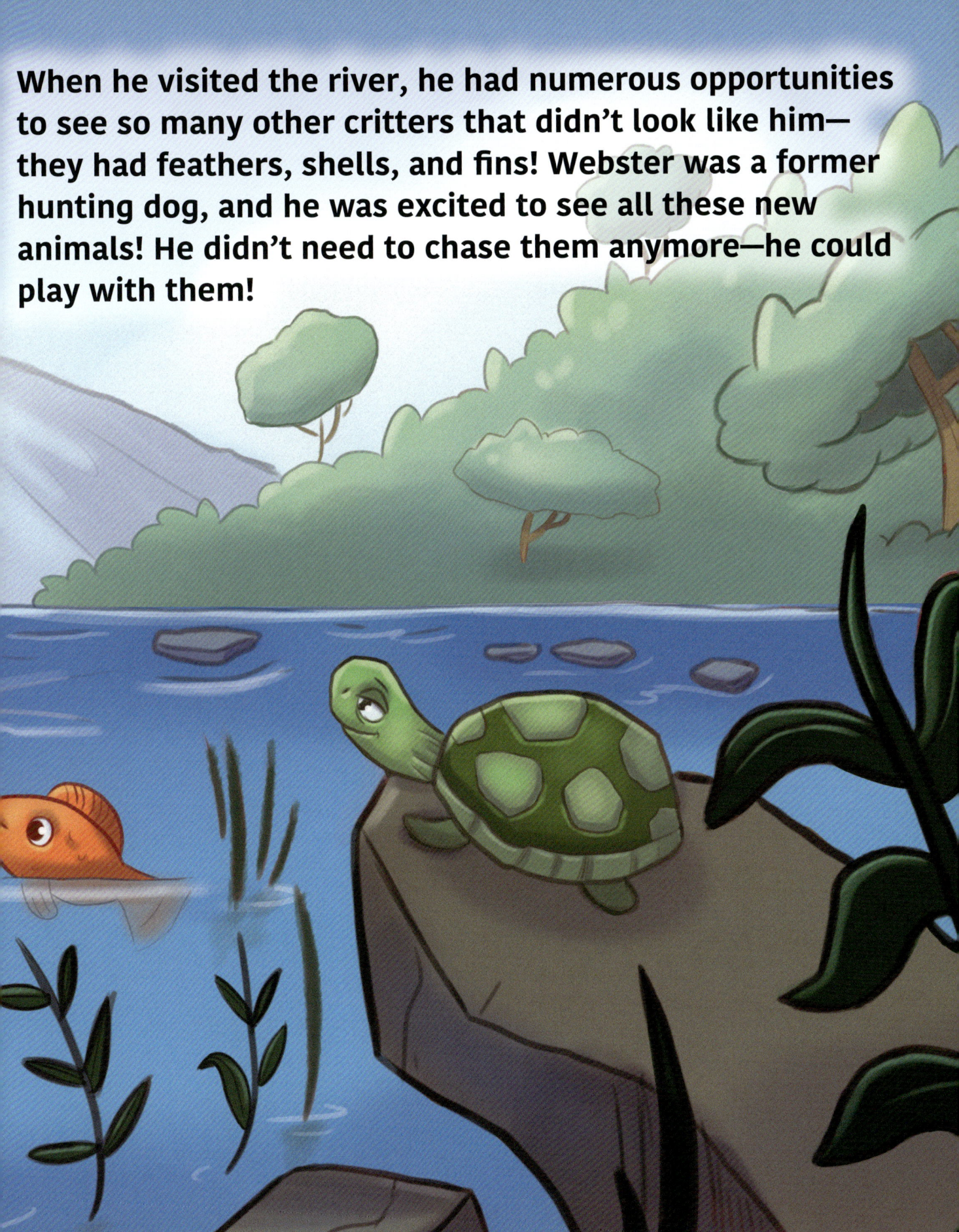

In the spring, Webster would venture down the pier to check on the ospreys in their nests. The same osprey couple came back every year to raise a new set of chicks.

Did You Know?

Did you know that Osprey can live up to twenty-five years? Their nickname is the "fish hawk" because their main diet consists of catching live fish and they don't need to drink water.

Ospreys mate for life and leave their river home in September, spend the winter in South America, and come back to the same place in March.

Ospreys build large nests out of sticks, trash, and even dog toys. The nest is placed on trees, cliffs, telephone and power poles, and manmade structures on the water.

In the summer, Webster's owner would take him crabbing on the boat, where they would haul in blue crabs from their own pots. One time, Webster got too close, and the crab gave him a little pinch!

Did You Know?

Did you know that blue crabs live along the East Coast of the United States, the Caribbean, and all the way down to South America—as far down as Argentina?

Female blue crabs only mate once in their lives and can have over two million eggs at a time! Blue crabs have ten legs, and the hind legs act as paddles.

Crabs can molt, which means they outgrow their bodies and shed their shells to grow bigger ones.

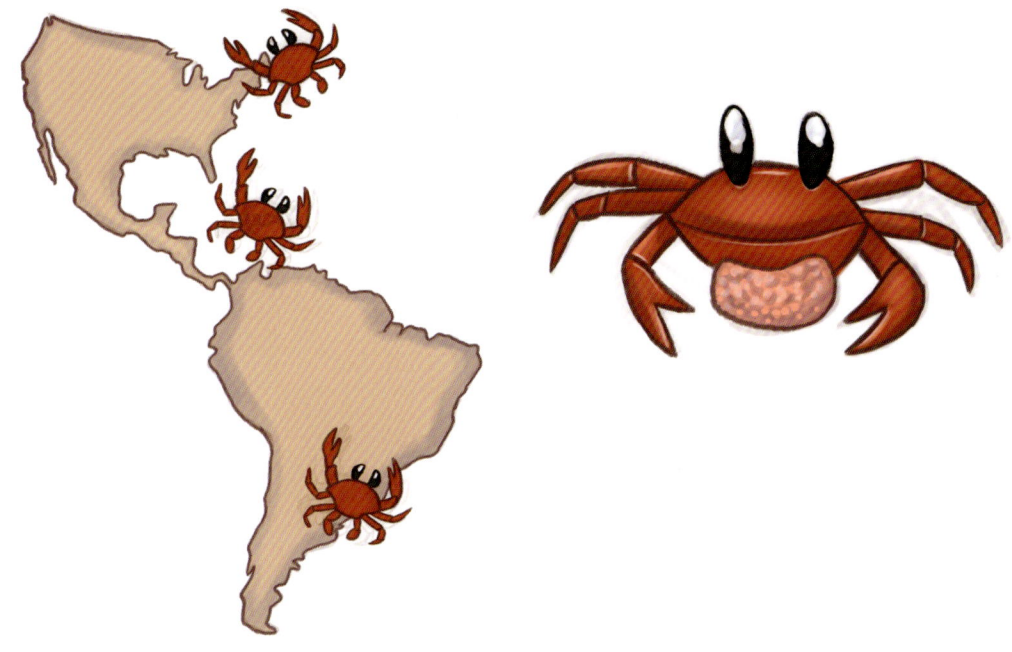

In the fall, Webster would go with his owner to harvest oysters from the river. He would oversee his owner collecting the oysters from his float and make sure everything was OK.

Did You Know?

Did you know that oysters have gills and breathe like fish? One oyster can filter fifty gallons of water a day!

Oysters can live up to twenty years and have been around for more than fifteen million years!

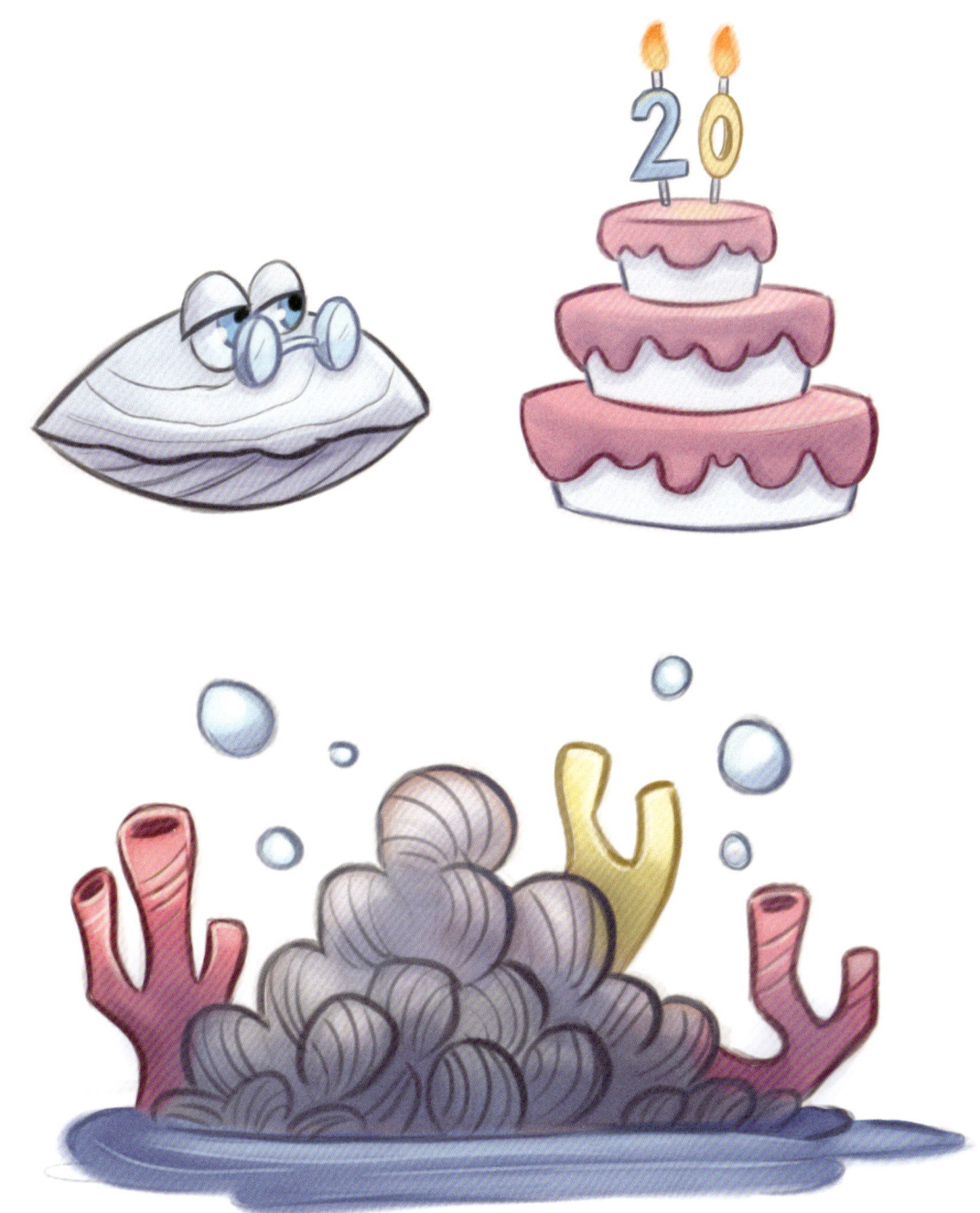

Natural oysters grow together and form reefs, providing shelter for crabs and small fish.

In early winter, Webster would be so excited . . . because that meant his owner would be loading him in the boat to go fishing for rockfish!

3 FEET

30 LBS

Did You Know?

Did you know that rockfish, or striped bass, live in the ocean but spawn in freshwater rivers? They can grow to be over three feet long, weigh as much as seventy pounds, and live to be thirty years old.

Rockfish mainly stay close to the shoreline and can live in both fresh water and salt water. There are limits on how many you can catch and what size they should be to protect them from being overfished.

When Webster would come back from fishing, he would wander over to the neighbors' porch where they would feed him fresh green beans. They loved Webster's visits because it brought them so much joy and comfort.

When Webster returned home from his journeys, he would take a nap in his very own hammock and enjoy the sunset with his brother, River the black lab.

Life at the river for Webster was so exciting, and he couldn't wait for all his adventures with birds, crabs, oysters, and fish. He loved running down the pier, being on the boat, napping, and watching the sunsets with his family.

In memory of my father, Togie Payne, who passed away in April 2023. He loved the river and is greatly missed.

About the Author

Frank's energy and enthusiasm are contagious, so dog breeds such as beagles and labradors are a perfect fit for him. He is an avid hunter, tennis player, and fan of all things James Madison University.

Frank is also active in his community and enjoys exploring new ventures—from owning racehorses to oyster farming. Frank is vice president and a minority owner of PD Brooks Company Inc., a traffic control company in Richmond, Virginia. He lives in Richmond with his wife, Caren, and their two dogs: Billy the beagle and River the black Labrador retriever.

On July 1, 2022, Frank adopted Billy the beagle from Richmond Animal Care Control (RACC). Billy was one of over four thousand beagles rescued from Envigo and adopted across the country. RACC was instrumental in protecting and fostering many of the beagles in Virginia.